Truck Pals on the Job

One Wrong Turn

written and illustrated by Ken Bowser

RED
CHAIR
•PRESS•™

Funny Bone Readers and Funny Bone Books are published by Red Chair Press
Red Chair Press LLC   PO Box 333   South Egremont, MA 01258-0333
www.redchairpress.com

For my Grandson, Liam Hayden Bowser
who never met a truck he didn't like.

Publisher's Cataloging-In-Publication Data
Bowser, Ken.

   One wrong turn / written and illustrated by Ken Bowser.

    pages : illustrations ; cm. -- (Funny bone readers. Truck pals on the job)

   Summary: All the parking meters have been checked for the day. It's time for Pam to head home. But when something goes wrong, will Pam be stuck on the freeway or will she get help getting back on the right road home?

   Interest age level: 004-008.

   ISBN: 978-1-63440-077-0 (library hardcover)

   ISBN: 978-1-63440-078-7 (paperback)

   Issued also as an ebook. (ISBN: 978-1-63440-079-4)

   1. Trucks--Juvenile fiction. 2. Helping behavior--Juvenile fiction. 3. Friendship--Juvenile fiction. 4. Trucks--Fiction. 5. Helpfulness--Fiction. 6. Friendship--Fiction. I. Title.

PZ7.B697 On 2016

[E]   2015938007

Printed in the United States of America
Distributed in the U.S. by Lerner Publisher Services. www.lernerbooks.com

1015 1P WRZSP16

Pam loved her little town. Its quiet
streets and narrow alleys were just right
for her. "This is my kind of place," Pam
thought as she checked the meters.

And she knew that her job as the town's Meter Reader was an important one. "Don't block any driveways, Dave!" she said to the big delivery truck.

"Not too close to the fire hydrant, Betty!"
she told the bread truck. "Careful not to
take up the handicapped spaces, Rod!"
she reminded the sports car.

Pam finished her rounds and headed home. She passed the bakery, the shoe shop, and the bank. Everyone waved as she passed by.

Then she came upon a new sign that she hadn't seen before. D-E-T-O-U-R it read. "Hmmm. Detour," Pam said to herself.

"A detour is when a road is closed for awhile for some reason," she thought to herself. "I guess I'll follow the detour signs for another way home."

"They must be repairing a pothole or a bump in the road," Pam said to herself. She turned left just as the detour sign directed.

"This is a pretty street," she thought as she turned again. "I've never been here before." Not paying attention, Pam took a right turn as she admired the street.

"Now this is an interesting little road,"
Pam said to herself as she began to climb.
"It's like a little hill. I like hills." Pam said.
"This should be fun!" she thought.

Suddenly, Pam found herself in a very
unfamiliar, VERY uncomfortable place!
The super highway! Before she knew it
Pam was swept up into the crazy traffic!

WHOOSH! Sports cars sped past with a WHIR! Big tractor-trailers blew by with a ROAR! "Uh-oh! This is not good!" she said.

The highway was so wide that Pam
could hardly tell where she should be!
"Where do I go? What do I do! I just
wanted to go home!" she complained.

It seemed like every other vehicle on the highway was bigger than Pam and going much faster than she dared to go. "Oh, I don't like this one bit!" Pam yelled.

There were giant bridges above her!
There were huge bridges below her!
Cars raced past her on the left.
Trucks blew past her on the right!

16

And it seemed there were confusing
signs everywhere she looked! Enter here!
Exit there! Merge this way! Merge that
way! Trucks stay to the right!

Pam tried to move over to the right but the traffic in that lane was moving too fast. She tried the left but the traffic in that lane was even faster!

Suddenly a huge tractor-trailer blew by Pam. The tailwinds spun her and tossed her off of the road where she stopped with a SKID!

Pam sat still for a moment catching her breath. "Whew! That was close!" she thought. Then she heard a voice. "Well shut my manifold!" the voice said.

20

Pam looked up and saw Tex the Road
Ranger truck. "You look lower than a little
old june-buggy!" Tex said. "I'm lost," said
Pam. "I just wanted to go home."

"Well old Tex will get you home quicker than you can say 'jumpin' jumper cables!" he said. Pam climbed aboard the big, safe truck and buckled herself in.

At last Pam was back on her own quiet
street. "I'm going to pay more attention to
the signs from now on!" she said to herself.
"Thanks for the lift, Tex!" she honked.

Big Questions: What happened that caused Pam to get on the wrong road home? How do you think she felt on the super highway?

Big Words:

detour: a change in the way traffic moves when a road is closed for awhile

highway: a wide main road between cities

tailwind: the rush of air blowing behind a moving truck